my town

written by Rebecca Treays

illustrated by Rachel Wells

digital artwork by Andrew Griffin

geography consultant: Rex Walford

senior designer: Non Figg; managing designer: Mary Cartwright; series editor: Felicity Brooks

This is my town. Lots of people live and work here. This picture shows some of the things you can find in my town.

Do you live in a town? Does your town have the same things in it as my town? What other things do you find in towns?

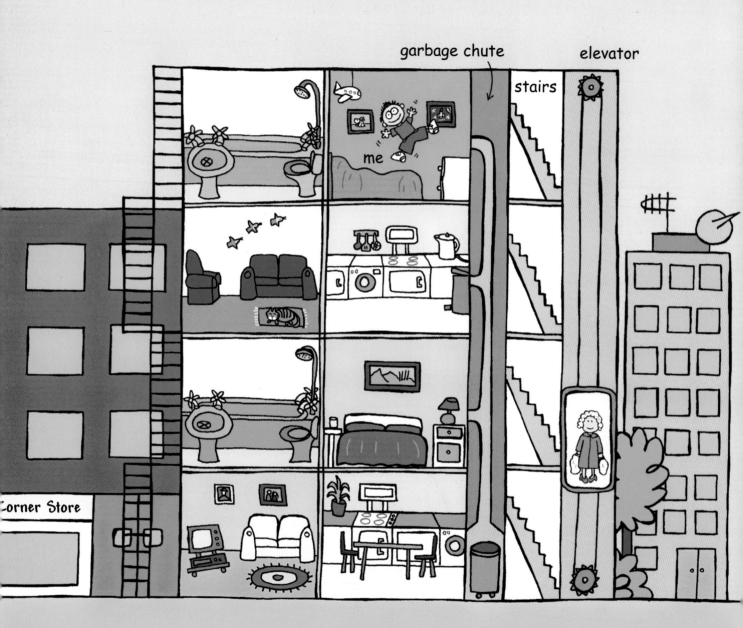

About 40 people live in my apartment building.

My apartment building has four floors. Some bigger towns have apartment buildings with more than thirty floors! What's the tallest building in your town?

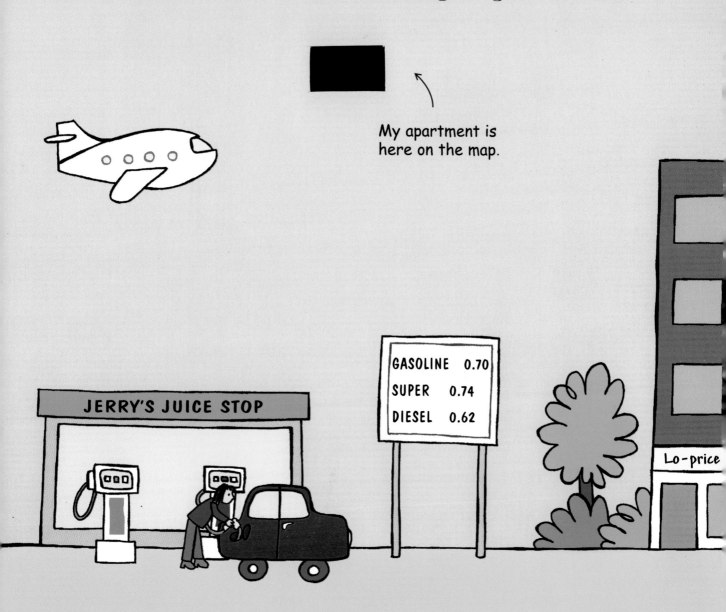

My apartment is here on the map.

JERRY'S JUICE STOP

GASOLINE   0.70
SUPER   0.74
DIESEL   0.62

Lo-price

I live in the middle of town in an apartment building. My apartment is on the top floor. Apartments save space, because homes are built on top of each other.

fire escape

my apartment

balcony

My friend Josie lives in the suburbs. The suburbs are at the edges of a town. There is more space to build big houses here. Josie's house has a yard and a garage.

Josie's house

garage

clothesline

swing

Groover

Josie lives in her house with her mom, dad, two brothers and her dog, Groover.

Every few years, the grown-ups in my town choose some people to run the town. They are called the town council.

The council works in this building called the town hall.

Everyone who works in the town pays money to the town council each year. This is called a tax.

The council decides how much money to spend on the things the town needs.

local buses and trains

schools and preschools

garbage pickups

QUIET

libraries and museums

parks and sports fields

What do you think towns should spend their money on? I'd like a new playground.

I am hardly ever bored in my town because there are so many things to do. On the weekends, Josie and I sometimes go to the swimming pool on Theater Street.

Now showing:
RETURN TO PLANET LOG
101 BEAVERS

swimming pool

Josie me

closed

In the summer, there is a carnival in my town. People dress up in costumes and parade along Main Street.

Can you see Josie, me and Groover in the crowd?

In my mom's office they make magazines.
Mom walks to work every day. Look at the map and see
if you can figure out how she could get to her office from
our apartment.

This is a building site. The builders are turning an old factory into apartments.

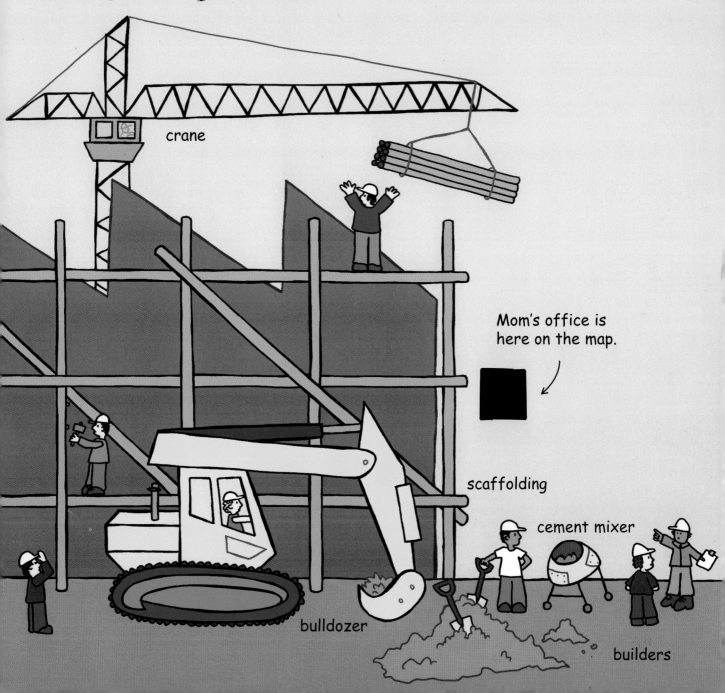

crane

Mom's office is here on the map.

scaffolding

cement mixer

bulldozer

builders

There are lots of jobs to do in my town. How many
different jobs can you spot people doing? Lift the flap
and you will see some more.

My mom works in
this office building.

SUNNYTOURS

star
buys

30¢

JOE'S TAXI

My dad works in a bank. Banks keep people's money safe for them. People who live in the country come into town to visit the bank.

150 years ago

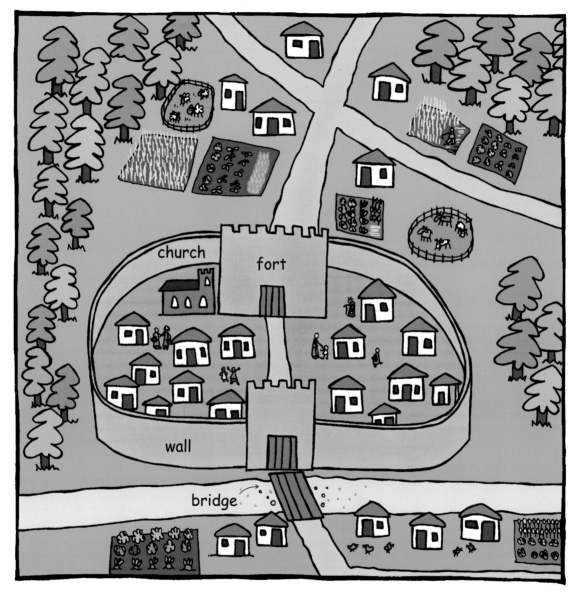

A fort was built on the hill. People came to live inside the fort walls where it was safe. There were a lot of battles between Native Americans and White settlers.

People built small houses and dug fields on a hill above the ford. They laid wooden planks by the ford to stop it from getting too muddy.

My town 300 years ago

300 years ago, my town was just a place on a river where it was shallow enough to cross. No people lived there. Look at the page opposite to see my town today.

My town today

This is my town now. Lift both flaps to see how it grew up over 300 years. As the town gets bigger, each picture shows more of the land around the ford.

50 years ago

big houses

park

river

More and more people moved into town. More stores were built. Some people moved into bigger houses in suburbs. The town council made some parks.

100 years ago

The fort has fallen down. Factories were built. Lots of people have come to town to work in them. They live in rows of small houses.

My town has lots of stores. My favorite is the pet store on Rufus Street. Can you find Rufus Street on the front map?

PETE'S PET STORE

girlie BOUTIQUE

open

my sister

On weekends, lots of people come into town, so the stores get really crowded.

Our superstore sells many different things. My sister always wants Mom to buy her new clothes. Can you see her in the store? Is there anything you can see in the superstore that you want to buy?

My apartment doesn't have a yard, but there is a big park nearby. I go there to play when it's sunny. Sometimes I take my bike.

hot dog stand

duck pond

gardener

picnic

skateboard ramp

There is a big superstore just outside my town. We drive there every Saturday and buy enough food for the whole week. Lift the flap to see inside.

The superstore has an enormous parking lot with enough space for hundreds of cars.

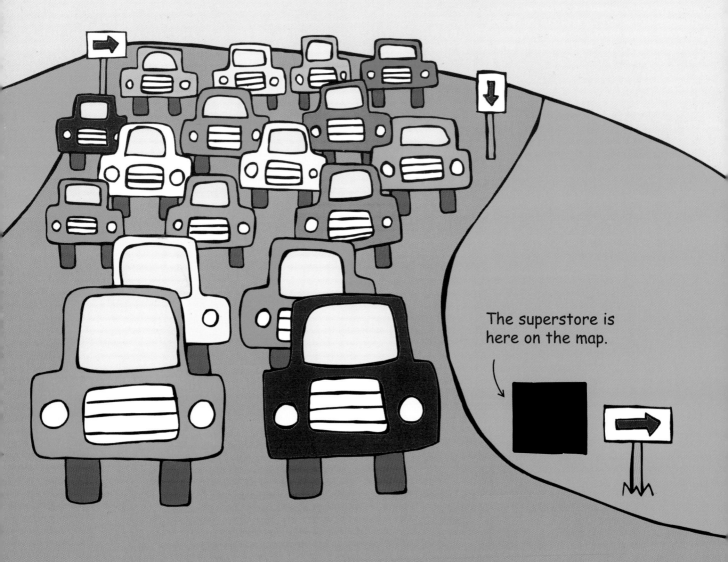

The superstore is here on the map.

Some people bring picnics and
spend all day in the park.

kites

caretaker

ice cream
seller

playground

sunbathers

trash
can

me

Josie

boating lake

On the map of my town, parks are shown in green.
Ponds and lakes are in blue. Can you find this park on
the front map? Remember it has a lake and a pond.

When we go out in the car, we often get stuck in traffic jams. Traffic jams are boring. It's the worst at rush hour, when people are going to work or coming home again.

Lift the flap to see what's causing the hold-up.

There is a big chocolate cookie factory in my town.

Lots of people who live in my town work here.

Cars and trucks aren't allowed in some parts of my town - only people and bikes. There are no traffic jams or smelly car fumes here.

Wells' Gifts

Figg's Cakes

Pedd Boo

stores

fountain

bike stands

sidewalk café

benches

Where is the bus going? Can you find that place on the back map? Who is getting hungry waiting for his pizza?

Josie and I want to work here when we grow up.
We want to be chief cookie tasters.

Choc'o'vat

TASTER

My town's chocolate cookies are famous
all over the world.

6:12
Nonningham
platform 2
Calling at:
Snorebridge
Rexington
Punterbury
Springfield
Burlington

6:19
Brookford
platform 4
Calling at:
Becsville
East Wheatley
Cartwright
Forest Glen

6:27
Marydale
platform 3
Calling at:
Tumton Wells
Springdale
Saffron Hill North
Littletown
Connersville

6:41
Hunters Beach
platform 1
Calling at:
West Brenda
Leatherford

6:11

20°C / 68°F

TRAINS OPERATED
BY SNAILTRACK . . .

TRACK SNACKS

Tickets and Information

closed

mail bags

This man has been shopping in town for a present.

Sometimes trains carry the mail.

The train station is one of the busiest places in my town.
There are always people coming and going.